# You're a Cow now

## Story by P.T. Mitchell · Art by Tony Gaddis

A MONSANTO DAIRY BUSINESS / CORE PROJECT

MONSANTO COMPANY / ST. LOUIS, MISSOURI

Library of Congress Control Number:   2003111236
ISBN 0-9744561-0-1

Printed in U.S.A.

First Edition, September, 2003

This book is dedicated to the values and work ethic
of America's dairy families. Who, generation after generation,
leave their land as healthy as they found it, provide wholesome
food for all, and treat their cows with care and respect.

Out in the country
    under the yellow sun,
there's a place where cows
live and work.
        It's called a Dairy Farm.

On this dairy there were
two-hundred cows in all
unless you count Moo Moo, the heifer,
which is a cow who is young,
then that would bring the total
to two-hundred and one.

The little cow saw a bird
  soar high overhead.
She asked a big cow,
"Will I ever be able to fly?"
  "Cows don't fly,"  the big cow said.

But I want to fly, thought Moo Moo.
I wish I was a bird high in the sky.
    I could flap my wings and sail.
And when it's cold and snowy,
    I'd be summering south
    in sunny Brazil.

Then a "bark!" and a "bark-bark!"
    Moo Moo heard.
She looked outside to see,
a dog quite pleased with himself
    was wrangling the herd.

A dog. Now that, thought the little cow,
is what I'd like to be.

"Big cow, I think I'd rather be a dog
    barking orders to heifers and cows.
It would be great fun
    to order everyone around.
I'd bark so loud they'd
    hear me in the nearby town."

"You'll never be a dog,"
    said the elder cow.
"Why such silly thoughts,
    especially now.
It causes me great alarm.
Don't you know, you're almost a big cow
and big cows get top billing on this farm?"

"But why do we stand about all day
        or eat or lay?
It's kind of boring, isn't it?
Is this living?
Going 'Moooo' all the time with
        a mouthful of feed with hay?"

"I'd rather be a dog
        or fly like a bird.
This life of chewing our cud,
        it's absurd.
I'd rather be a bee
or go 'ribbit!' like a frog
        than be another cow in the herd!"

"Shhhhhh!" said the big cow
as the rest of the herd looked at Moo Moo.

They were not amused.

Then the farmer came and
led the cows out of the barn,
down a hall and into a big clean room.
"Come along," said the big cow.

"There's something I want you to see."
The cows each stood in a stall,
    Moo Moo too.

Gently and swiftly,
the farmer put the milking hoses
on the udder of every cow.
The big cow said to Moo Moo,
"You'll see who's the boss now."

With a "Moooo" as the signal
    the milk began to flow.
Moo Moo was surprised to be milking too.
Who knew she had
    all this milk stored below?
So much milk the cows made so quickly,
    it was a spectacular show.

"See all this milk?" said the big cow.

"It is more precious than gold.
It feeds babies, children,
the young and the old.
I can make over thirty-thousand pounds
of milk a year.
Or feed roughly 75 people a day.
That's a lot of milk and cheese and yogurt
either way."

"As natural as natural can be
and as important to health
        as the air that we breathe.
This magical drink,
        it's made thanks to big cows like me.
And the hard work and pampering
        from our good farmer, Farmer Steve."


"I see," said Moo Moo.

After milking, they lay down
　　　on freshly made beds.
The big cow said,
"Let me tell you a secret,
　　　my little heifer and a half.
There's lots of animals on this big earth.
　　　But why envy the neck of a giraffe?
Don't look for what you don't have,
when all you need is right here at home."

"Besides,
    anyone who knows anything knows
us dairy cows are the greatest of all."

    "I completely agree," said Moo Moo.
"Good. Oh, and by the way,
welcome to the herd," said the big cow.

    "So I'm a cow now?"
"You're a cow now."


    "YIPPEE!"

"Just remember,
if you want to be great,
    don't look at what you're missing.
You don't have to run like a dog,
fly south with the birds
    or try to cackle like a chicken."

"Make the most of what you've got.
It's easy to find.
  It's the thing you were meant to be.
All you have to do is just do what you do
  most naturally."